NINA STREISAND

Sher

LITTLE IS NICE

LITTLE IS NICE

by
ALICIA
KAUFMANN

pictures by
VICTORIA
de
LARREA

Hawthorn Books, Inc.

Publishers   New York

For Darius and Noel, and their daddy

First Edition: 1970

Nicky didn't like anything to
be little.

When his grandmother
bought him a balloon in the
park, he made sure he picked
the biggest one in the bunch.
Then he would hold on to the
end of the string and stretch his
neck up toward the sky to see
how far his very big balloon
could reach.

That's the way Nicky was
about everything. He always
chose big carrots, big apples, big
cookies. He wanted big blocks
to build with, a big bunch of
crayons, a big stack of paper.
He wanted only big toys. If
anyone gave him and his brother
toys, Nicky would look carefully
to make sure his were not
smaller.

Nicky's parents had a little car. Nicky liked his friend Jeannie's big station wagon better. "Why do we have such a little car?" he wanted to know.

"Because a little car is nice," his mother answered. "It can squeeze into little places and wiggle in and out of traffic. We chose a little car because we liked it best of all."

"Well, I still like big cars better," Nicky said.

Sometimes Nicky's father would say, "I'll play with you for a little while."

"No," Nicky would answer, "it has to be a big while!"

Nicky had a green tricycle
with a loud bell and colored
streamers on the handlebars. He
could ride very fast on it—
backward and forward, uphill
and downhill, over grass and
bumps.

Then his older brother, Jay, got a new two-wheeler.

Nicky looked at the new bike for a long time. He watched his brother climb up on the high seat and stretch his long legs out to reach the pedals.

Nicky started to cry. "I don't like my green bike. It's too little."

Nicky's father said, "When you get bigger you can have a bigger bike, too." But that only made Nicky feel worse.

Most of all, Nicky didn't like being little himself.

People were always telling him how much he was growing. Even Jay noticed the way he could reach the high buttons on the elevator now, and said, "Wow! Look how big Nicky is getting."

His friend Jeannie thought he
was big, too, because he was
such a fast runner. And while he
was running, he felt very big.
But that wasn't enough. Nicky
still knew he was the littlest
person in his family. And he
didn't like it.

Nicky watched his father put on his great big coat and wished he could be big like him. "Why are daddies so big?" he asked.

His father answered, "They've had a long time to grow. When you grow up you'll be big, too."

"When I grow up I'll be a giant!" Nicky laughed.

At Halloween, Nicky and his
brother were going to play trick
or treat. Jay made himself a
monkey mask, but Nicky said, "I
want to be the biggest animal in
the world."

"How about a giraffe?" his
brother suggested. "That's taller
than anything." And with a little
help from his mother, and a
long broom, and a paper bag to
hide his face, Nicky became
a giraffe.

"Hey, look at me!" he shouted.
"I'm as high as the sky."

When they rang the bell of the house next door, a plump, smiling lady opened it. She started to laugh when she saw the children. "Look at those funny creatures! Who could they be?"

"Trick or treat!" shouted the two funny creatures.

"Aha!" said the lady. "I've got an idea. I'll give one of you a trick and I'll give the other one a treat."

First she gave both boys a lollipop. Then she put a bundle wrapped in shiny paper in Jay's hand, and another, tiny, bundle in Nicky's hand.

When Nicky got home he was crying so hard his tears were wetting the paper around his face. "I got a tiny one," he sniffed.

"A tiny what?" his mother
asked.

"I don't know, but it's so
little," Nicky answered.

"Well, let's open it and see."
His mother was getting curious.

So Nicky took a peek anyway,
and a sniff, and a lick. He could
tell it was a piece of sweet
chocolate and he really loved
chocolate.

Then Nicky's brother started to open his package. It felt round and hard, and everyone thought it was going to be a jellied apple or a juicy orange or . . . And everyone was wrong. It was a dusty old raw potato! That was the trick!

At first Jay didn't think it was so funny, but then he started laughing along with the others. And Nicky just couldn't help saying, "I'm glad I got the little one."

When it was time to go to bed, they were still laughing. Nicky laughed so much his stomach hurt. "Does it hurt a lot or a little?" his father asked. "Oh, just a little," Nicky answered.

"Hurray!" yelled his brother. "A little stomach ache is better than a big one!"

The next day the two boys
went to the library with their
mother. Nicky usually took
home the biggest books he could
find. But this day was different.
He looked at some fat books,
some tall ones and some heavy
ones. And he did not choose
any of them.

Then he saw a little book,
with little pictures of a little
boy. Nicky held it in his hands.
He opened the book and closed
it again. It was nice—and that
was the book Nicky took home.